To
Francis
Nicdao
—M. J.

Text copyright © 2010 by Harriet Ziefert
Illustrations copyright © 2010 by Mark Jones
All rights reserved / CIP Data is available.
Published in the United States 2010 by ⬤ Blue Apple Books
515 Valley Street, Maplewood, NJ 07040
www.blueapplebooks.com
First Edition   Printed in China 03/10
ISBN: 978-1-60905-015-3
1 2 3 4 5 6 7 8 9 10

Distributed in the U.S. by Chronicle Books

Harriet Ziefert

Butterfly
Birthday

ILLUSTRATED BY

Mark Jones

🍎 BLUE APPLE BOOKS

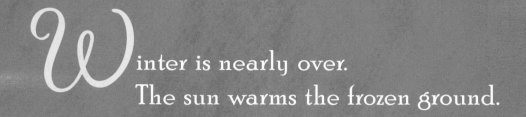

Winter is nearly over.
The sun warms the frozen ground.

Purple crocuses are the first to announce the coming of spring.

Beetles and crickets emerge
from their winter hiding places.

Worker ants unblock
the entrance to their colony.

Bug friends greet each other
after many cold months.

"It's been too long!"
says Stripey Beetle.

"Yes . . . long, dark nights,"
agrees Fuzzy Caterpillar.

Now is the time the insects prepare for a party
to celebrate the first day of spring.

Wasps make wax pots and spiders spin
bags of silk to help the ones who will
gather food for the celebration.

The ants work hard to find
tasty tidbits to fill the food containers.

One little ant is angry.
He shouts to three busy caterpillars,
"If you keep eating and don't do work,
then you can't have any treats at the party!"

A cardinal returning from warmer weather
notices the activity, but leaves the insects alone.
Even he knows this is a special day.

Once the food is gathered,
the insects dress up for the party.
They put on hats, ties, necklaces—
even a mask.

"You look splendid," says Cricket.

"So spiffy," says Little Ant.

"Really spiffy!" says Big Ant.

Grandma Beetle takes Little Ant aside.
She points to several delicately-colored
chrysalises, flecked with golden dots.

"The caterpillars were not just busy munching leaves," says Grandma Beetle. "They gave us decorations for our party."

"But where did the caterpillars go?" asks Little Ant.

"When the party is over, you will know," answers Grandma Beetle.

At midday, the feast begins.
Big Click Beetle is the dinner speaker.
He welcomes everyone to the celebration.

"Today is one of only two days in the year when there are exactly twelve hours of day and twelve hours of night. Both day and night are equal, and so this date is called the vernal equinox."

Big Click turns everyone's attention
to the hanging chrysalises.

"Butterflies are struggling to break out.
Let's watch them, then sing Happy Birthday."

Little Ant says,
"Now I get it.
The caterpillars wrapped
themselves in chrysalises,
then presto change~o,
they became butterflies.
It's magic!"

"Not magic,"
answers Big Cricket.
"Metamorphosis!"

The butterflies pump fluid
into their crumpled wings
so that they spread out.
They move their wings
slowly at first, and then
faster as their wings dry.

Everyone watches
in silence—too astonished
to make a sound.

Amazing!

The band plays classical insect music.

When they are ready, the butterflies
take flight. Everyone buzzes with delight.

The sun hangs low in the sky.

While insects dance atop the mushroom, butterflies dance in the air.

As night falls, moths emerge
from their cocoons
and join the celebration.

Fireflies illuminate
the festivities.

The butterflies thank the other insects
for a beautiful birthday party.
"It's time for us to go. Good night."

Beetle waves
as Monarch flutters
her wings in a
silent good-bye.

So ends the first day of spring.

Over the next few weeks there will be many other birthdays
until the new season is in full bloom.

All is quiet—except for one last question from Little Ant.

"Where do butterflies go when
they are tired and want to sleep?"